A Kid's Cat Library™

Persian Cats

Jennifer Quasha

The Rosen Publishing Group's
PowerKids Press™
New York

For Teddy

Published in 2000 by The Rosen Publishing Group, Inc.
29 East 21st Street, New York, NY 10010

Copyright © 2000 by The Rosen Publishing Group, Inc.

First Edition

Book Design: Michael de Guzman

Photo Credits: pp. 1, 15, 20 © Fritz Prenzel/Animals Animals; pp. 4, 19 © Robert Maier/Animals Animals; pp. 7, 12, 16, 22 © Henry Ausloos/Animals Animals; p. 8 © Terence Gili/Animals Animals and © 1996 Andromedia Interactive Ltd; p. 11 © Robert Pearcy/Animals Animals and © Keystone View Co./FPG International.

Quasha, Jennifer.
    Persian cats / by Jennifer Quasha.
        p.   cm. — (A kid's cat library)
    Includes index.
    Summary: Relates the history of the Persian cat and describes the physical and other characteristics of this quietest and least active of all cat breeds.
    ISBN 0-8239-5508-7
    1. Persian cat—Juvenile literature. [1. Persian cat. 2. Cats.] I. Title. II. Series: Quasha, Jennifer. Kid's cat library.
SF449.P4Q36 1999
636.8'32—dc21

                                                                                        98-53564
                                                                                        CIP
                                                                                        AC

Manufactured in the United States of America

Contents

This Persian kitten will grow up to be a very affectionate pet.

The Beautiful Persian

Persian cats are famous for their long, soft fur. These fluffy pets are the quietest and least active of all cat **breeds**. Persians like to stay inside and curl up in warm places. They are very loving cats and show lots of **affection** to their owners. There are almost fifty different colors and patterns of Persian cats. No matter what color or pattern their fur comes in, these cats are known for their beautiful **coats**.

Persian Cats in War

Persian cats came from a country in the Middle East that used to be called Persia. Today it is Iran. In 525 B.C., the Persians were fighting the Egyptians for land. The Egyptians believed cats to be **sacred**. It was illegal in Egypt to hurt a cat. The Persians knew this.

There is even a story that when the Persians went into battle against the Egyptians, they attached cats to their shields. The Persians knew that when the Egyptians saw the cats, they wouldn't use their weapons. They wouldn't want to hurt the sacred cats. According to this story, the Persians won the battle because of the cats.

Whether or not this story is true, Persian cats have won the hearts of people around the world. ▶

Russia

Iran
(Persia)

China

Saudi Arabia

India

Philippines

Breed History

Persian cats were first brought from Persia to Italy in 1620 by an Italian traveler named Pietro della Valle. At the same time, another man named Nicholas-Claude Fabri de Peirese brought Persian cats to France. At first, Persians were **bred** only in Europe. They were very popular among rich people. To own a Persian cat was rare and very special. Soon their popularity grew. Over hundreds of years, Persian cats spread throughout Europe.

◀ *You don't have to be rich to own a Persian today.*

Queen Victoria

Queen Victoria was the queen of England from 1837 to 1901. She loved Persian cats and had some of her own. She owned very pretty, bluish-gray cats called blue Persians. Blue Persians were Queen Victoria's favorite. The queen owned blue Persians, so people all around Europe wanted to own them too. For a short time, **breeders** would breed only blue Persians because that was the only color people wanted to buy. It was very difficult to find brown, orange, or **tabby** Persians at that time.

Persian cats are so popular today that you can find one with almost any color and fur pattern that you can think of.

The Persian Comes to America

In 1885, a brown tabby Persian named King Humbert was brought to the United States. He may have been the first Persian brought to the United States. Until this point, the Maine coon cat had been the favorite long-haired cat in the United States. The Persian became very popular, very quickly. Soon, it was more popular than the Maine coon.

In 1930, the **Cat Fanciers' Association** awarded a Persian cat the title of Grand Champion. This was the highest award ever given to a cat at a cat show. The winner's name was Eastbury Trigo. He was a red tabby Persian.

These red tabby Persian kittens may grow up to be champions too.

The Look of the Persian

The Persian cat looks different than many other breeds of cats. It has a large, fluffy head and small, rounded ears. The Persian's face looks kind of pushed in. It has a shorter nose than many other kinds of cats. Persians have fluffy, well-rounded bodies that make them look fatter than they really are. Most of their size comes from their long, thick fur.

Persians have beautiful eyes that are usually copper, green, **hazel**, or blue. Breeders have found that white Persians with blue eyes are often deaf. Persians may also have eyes of two different colors. Some Persians with a blue eye and an eye of another color are deaf in the ear that is closest to the blue eye.

Copper eyes, like this cat's, are a common eye color for Persians. ▶

Grooming

Since Persians have so much fur, it is easy for their fur to get tangled. It is important to **groom** a Persian every day. To groom a Persian you need a comb and a brush. First, comb the fur gently, making sure to get out all the knots. Then brush the cat. If there are lots of tangles, you can sprinkle some **talcum powder** on the fur. Powder helps the brush get through the tangles.

It takes a lot of work to keep a Persian looking shiny and beautiful.

Cat Tales

Have you ever heard the expression, "a cat has nine lives"? Well, cats don't really have nine lives. That expression started in Egypt. The Egyptians believed that the number nine had magical powers. They connected that with cats, because they believed that cats were close to the **gods**.

Other people say that cats have nine lives because they seem to get through tough situations without getting hurt. Cats can **survive** falls, bad weather, and living outdoors for weeks or months. Other pets may not be able to survive these things.

Persians are happiest curled up in a warm, protected place. However, their thick fur coat would allow them to survive outside in cold weather.

Smart Cats

Persian cats may sometimes seem lazy. They like to cuddle and sleep more than anything else. However, Persians are very smart. They can find their way home even from a long distance. A Persian cat once walked 1,500 miles to find her owner. It took the cat thirteen months to make the trip. Walking that distance is like walking halfway across the United States. This cat found food and warm places to sleep during the trip. She was smart enough and **determined** enough to find her owner.

◀ *Persians feel very close to their owners.*

21

A Favorite Pet

Persians are the most popular cats in the United States today. They have been popular since they arrived here more than 100 years ago. Persians are so well-loved because they are beautiful, calm pets. They are friendly and love to play with children.

Learning how to care for the long coat of the Persian takes a little time. Once you learn, you will have a loving, happy cat. Happy cats are the best pets.

Web Sites:

http://www.cas.american.edu/~hmann/Map/menell /index.html

http://www.worldkids.com/critters/pets/cats/ persian.htm

Glossary

affection (uh-FEK-shun) Showing lots of love.

bred (BRED) When people have brought a male and female animal together so that they would have babies.

breed (BREED) A type of animal.

breeder (BREE-der) A person who brings a male and female animal together so they will have babies.

Cat Fanciers' Association (KAT FAN-see-erz uh-SOH-see-AY-shun) A group that organizes cat shows and makes sure that cat breeders breed healthy cats.

coat (COHT) An animal's fur.

determined (dih-TER-mihnd) Being very focused on a goal.

god (GOD) A being that is thought to have more power than humans.

groom (GROOM) To bathe and care for the coat and nails of an animal.

hazel (HAY-zul) A brownish, greenish color.

sacred (SAY-kred) Highly respected and considered very important.

survive (ser-VYV) To stay alive.

tabby (TA-bee) A striped and spotted pattern on a cat's fur.

talcum powder (TAL-kum POW-der) A powder for the body.

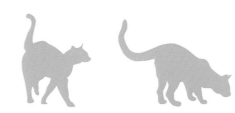

Index